Contents

Learn the Canon EOS Digital Rebel Camera for 5 Bucks

Stephen Gregory

Fair Shake Press, an imprint of Pearson Technology Group, division of Pearson Education

Composed in the typeface Cronos MM from Adobe Systems

ISBN 0-321-28782-7

9 8 7 6 5 4 3 2 1

Printed and bound in the United States of America

How to use this book

Welcome to a new way of learning cool high-tech products, like the Canon Digital Rebel Camera. What I wanted to do with this book is something that has probably never been done before (at least not with the Rebel), and that is to take this incredibly powerful camera and make it incredibly easy to use. In reality, the Rebel—just like all the cameras in Canon's Digital EOS line—*is* very easy to use—you just have to know where to look to accomplish what you want. Showing exactly that—and nothing more—is my goal. I simply want to show you, one-on-one, how to do the things that you (and almost everybody else) want to do with the Canon Rebel digital camera, and nothing more.

I'm not going to talk about how to compose a photo, or get into the intricacies of exposure compensation or debate the virtues of traditional vs. digital formats. Also, I won't go deeply into care and maintenance issues, such as how to clean your lens, and adjusting the sensors, and stuff like that. Those topics are already in the manual that came with your camera, so you'd probably rather get right into the fun stuff, right? Right! I'm just going to show you exactly how to do the most requested, most important, and most useful things with the Rebel so you can start shooting and having fun with it right away. Today!

Now, although the official name of the camera is the Canon EOS Digital Rebel camera, if I called it that every time I referred to it, you'd want to strangle me by the end of the book, so most of the time I just call it the Digital Rebel, or occasionally just the Rebel.

So grab your Rebel, turn the page, and start learning how to use one of the coolest cameras ever made.

—Stephen Gregory

How to charge the battery

> *Might as well do this first*

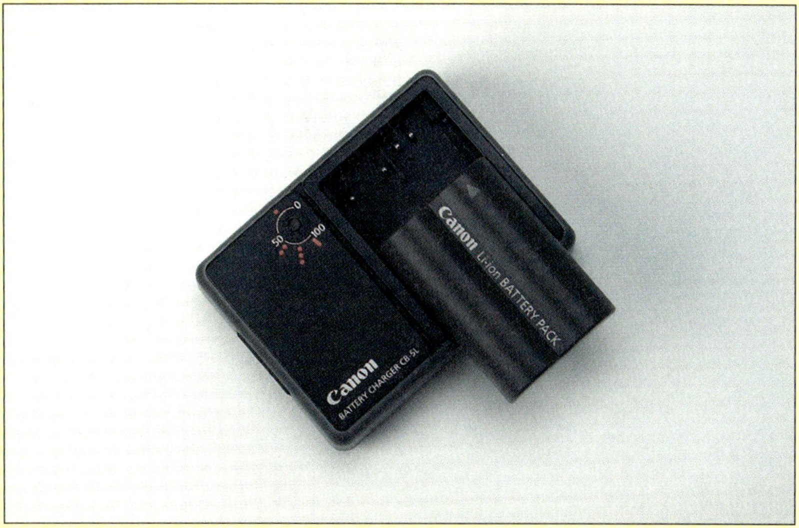

The Canon Digital Rebel comes with a separate battery charger. You should probably charge up the battery now before you dive into learning the camera. To charge the battery, first connect the power cord to the charger and plug the battery charger into the wall. Then slide the battery into the battery pack slot (the arrow on the battery shows the direction the battery should be inserted into the charger). On the charger itself there's a little round red light that tells you how much charge the battery has. A solid red light means the battery is fully charged. If the red light blinks on/off three times in 1 second, it means the battery has between a 75% and 90% charge. If it blinks twice in 1 second, it means the battery has a 50–75% charge. If it blinks once every second, it means the charge is below 50% and it's time to hook up the charger.

Where the battery goes in your Digital Rebel

> *The battery compartment is under the camera*

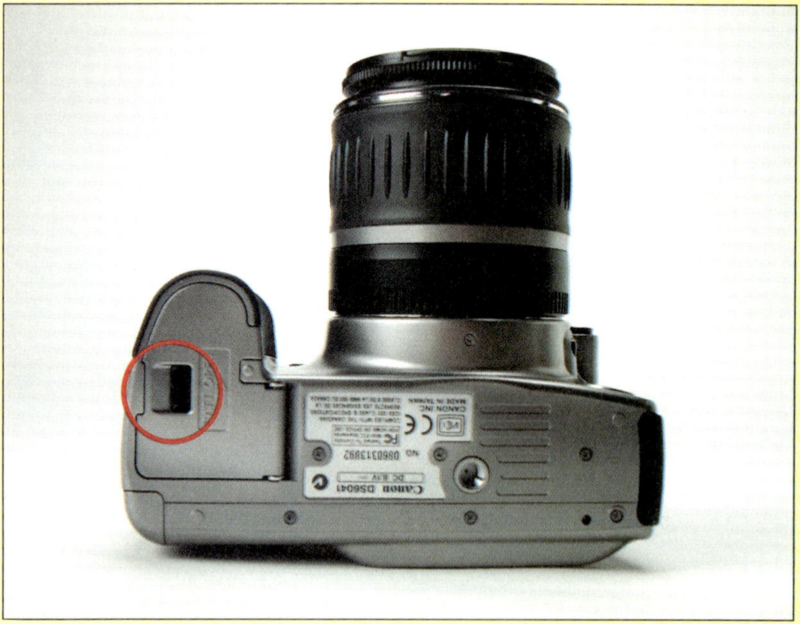

If you turn the Digital Rebel upside down, you'll see a large black compartment door. That's where the battery goes. So slide the little tab over, and the door will pop open. Slide the battery in with the arrow facing downward into the compartment until it snaps into place. Needless to say, don't force the battery into the compartment—it should be a snug fit, but if you're having to force it, you're probably trying to put it in backward or upside down, which will damage either the battery or the camera, so forcing it is never a good idea. If you need to remove the battery, look in the same place. There's a little orange tab you have to pull back that holds the battery in place. Pull it back and the battery pops out.

Turning on the camera

> *And how to know if it's turned on*

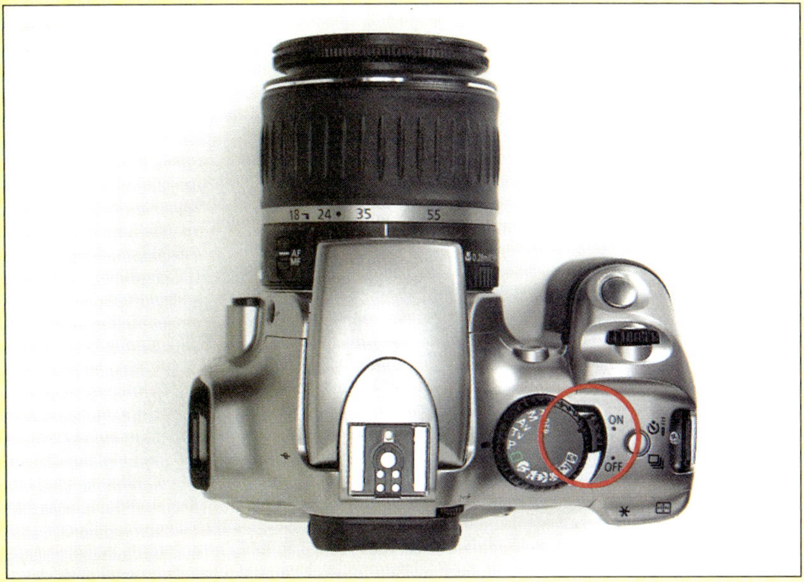

To turn on your Digital Rebel, move the knob on the round slider on the top of the camera to the On position (this round slider is right next to the Shutter Release button). You'll know whether the camera is on or not by taking a quick peek at the back of the camera, right above the color LCD monitor. If it's on, you'll see information appearing in this gray LCD readout area (don't look at the preview—where you see your photos displayed—look just above that). If you see info, it's on.

How to insert your memory card

> *Think of this as putting the film in your camera*

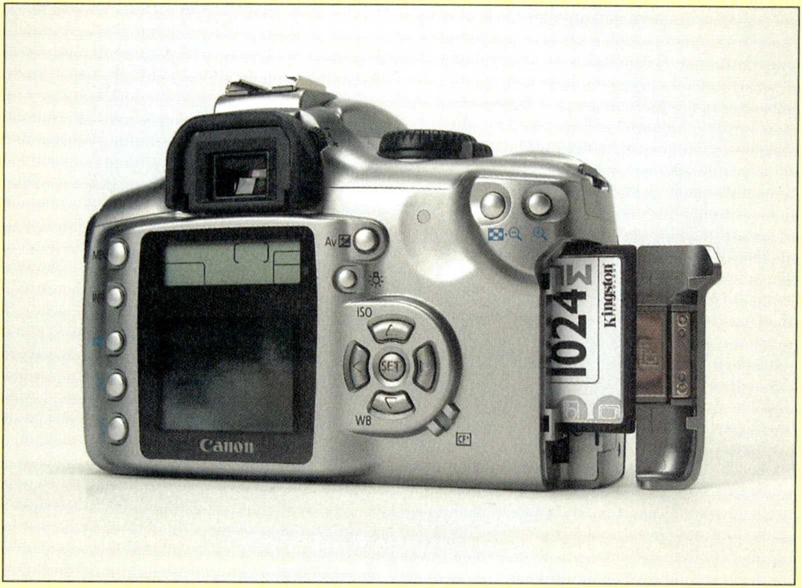

Think of your memory card as the film for your camera, because essentially that's what it is. The type of "film" used by the Digital Rebel is called "CompactFlash" (CF for short) memory, so if you want to buy more "digital film" make sure you ask for a CompactFlash memory card. Cards comes in a variety of sizes (64 MB, 128 MB, 256 MB, 512 MB, 1 GB, 2 GB, and on up). The larger the amount of memory, the more photos the card will hold, so most folks try to buy as large a card as they can afford. To insert the memory card into the camera, first turn the camera off, then slide open the cover on the side of the camera (as shown here), and slip the card right in (there's a little arrow on the label of the card that shows you which direction the card goes in). Then snap the cover closed.

Formatting your memory card for the Digital Rebel

> *You've got to do this the first time you use the memory card*

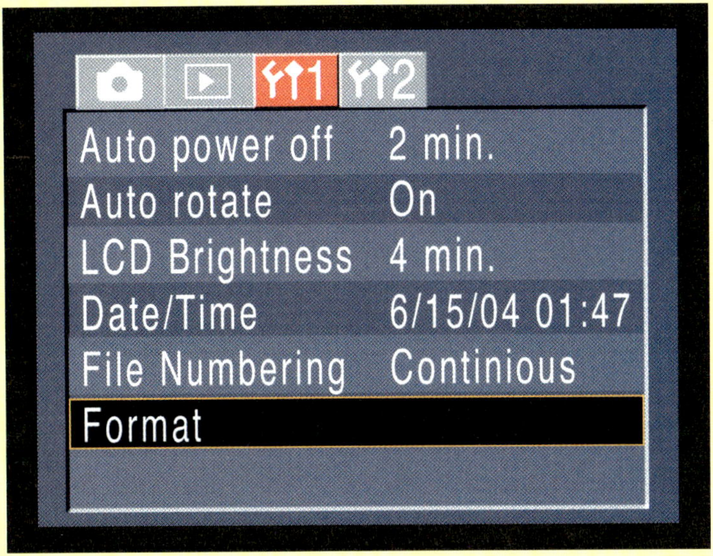

The first time you use your CompactFlash memory card, you have to format the card so it knows it's being used by a Canon Digital camera. Luckily, this is a no-brainer because the camera does it for you—you just have to tell the camera to do the formatting. Press the Menu button on the back of the camera, then press the right arrow button twice to scroll over to the Set-up 1 Menu. Press the Set button, then use the down arrow button to scroll down to Format (as shown above), and press Set again to format your card. A word of caution: Formatting erases the entire contents of the card (in other words, it deletes every photo). So you only want to format a CompactFlash card either first time you use it or when you actually want to delete every photo and start over with an empty card. There is no "undo" for formatting, so make sure it's what you really want to do.

How to change your lens

> *If you've got more than one lens, here's how to swap them out*

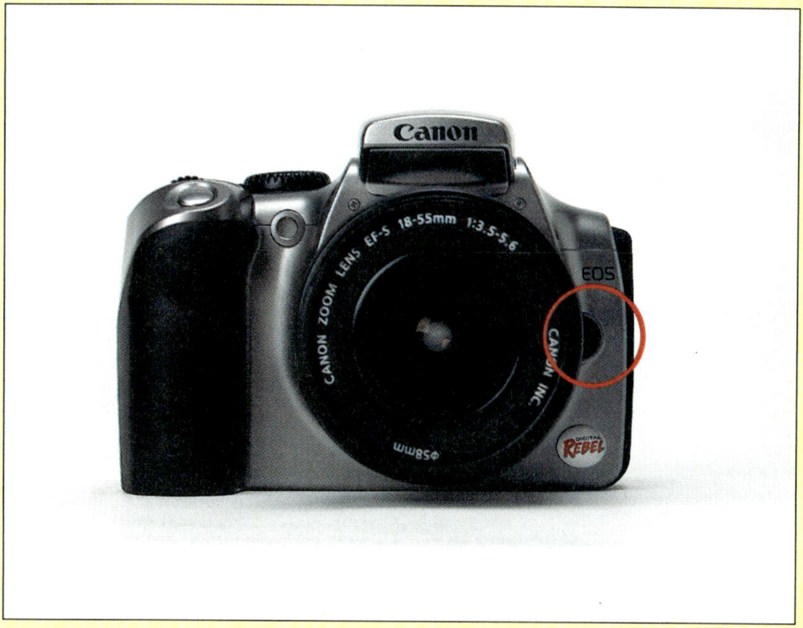

If you've got more than one lens (which is one of the main advantages of using a digital SLR like the Rebel—you can change lenses) and you want to change lens, it's pretty straightforward. Start by removing the lens that's attached to the camera body by holding the Lens Release button on the front of the camera, just to the right of the lens (as shown above). Then put your hand around the lens and turn it slowly in a counterclockwise rotation, and the lens will "unscrew." Now take your other lens, line up the white alignment dot on the lens with the white dot on the camera body, and turn the lens in a clockwise rotation until it locks into place. See, I told you it was straightforward.

Setting the Auto Power Off timer

> *If you don't set this, the camera will turn off in one minute automatically*

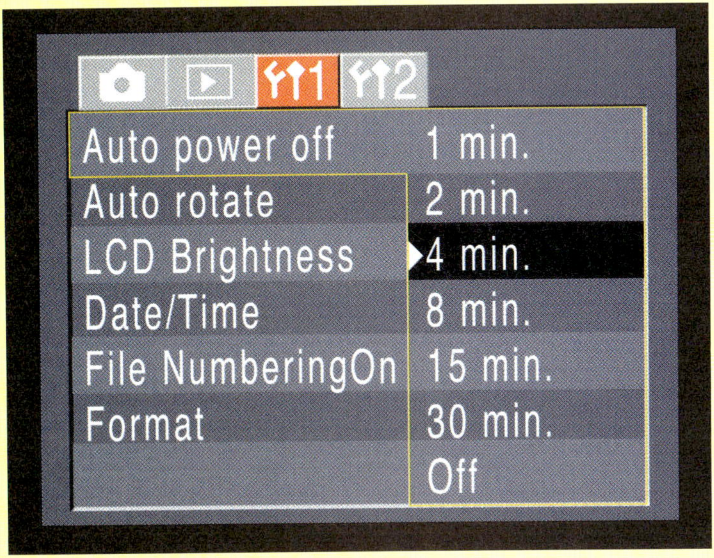

To help save battery life, the Rebel has an Auto Power Off feature that automatically turns the camera off after 1 minute of inactivity. So if you're shooting a race and take a few shots as the cars zoom past, by the time they come around for the next lap, even on a small track, the camera already will have shut itself off and you'll miss the shot. This drives people (mostly my wife) crazy because they miss a lot of great shots. Luckily, you can change the amount of time the Rebel waits until it turns itself off. Press the Menu button on the back of the camera, then use the right arrow button to scroll over to Set-up Menu 1. Press the down arrow button, and the top item in this menu (Auto power off) will be highlighted. Press the Set button, then use the down arrow button to choose a length of time before the camera auto powers off, then press the Set button to lock it in.

Navigating the menu on the back of the camera

> *There are two different ways—the arrow buttons or the main dial*

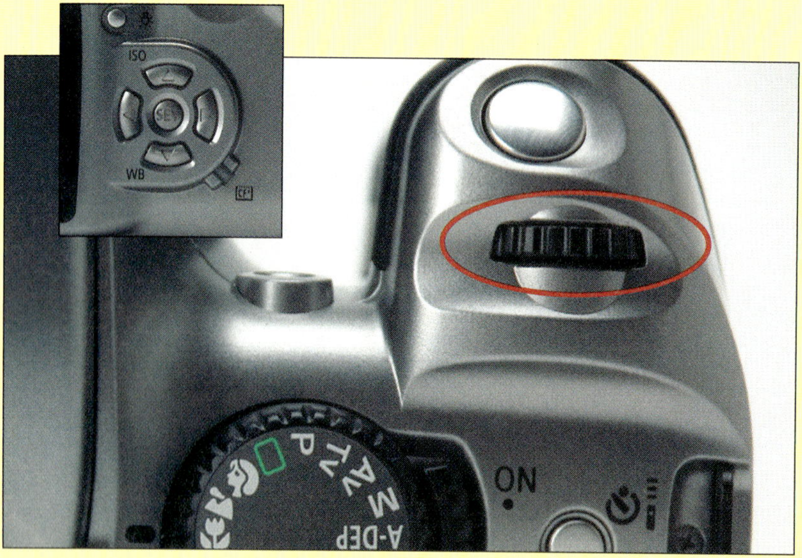

On the previous page, you used the arrow buttons on the back of the camera to navigate through the menus that appear on the color LCD monitor. Although you will need the left/right arrow buttons to choose which menu you want to be in (Camera, Play, Set-up Menu 1 or Set-up Menu 2), once you've found the menu you want, you can use the Main Dial (which is located on the top of the camera, right behind the Shutter button) to scroll up and down within that menu. However, I still recommend using the arrow buttons, because once you find the menu item you want, you still have to press the Set button to make your selection, and the Set button is in the center of the arrow buttons (shown inset above). So if your hand is already on the arrow buttons, it just makes getting to the Set button that much easier.

Waking the camera from sleep (auto off)

> *Just press the Shutter button and the camera wakes right up*

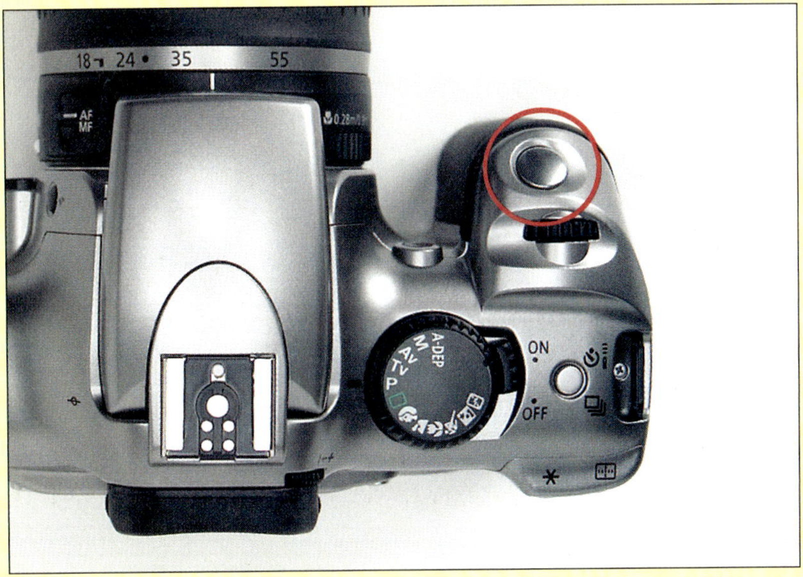

To conserve your battery power, the Digital Rebel has an Auto Power Off function that automatically turns the camera off after a minute of nonactivity. To wake the camera again, just lightly press the Shutter button (as shown above).

How to take a shot

> *If you can push a button, you can take a shot*

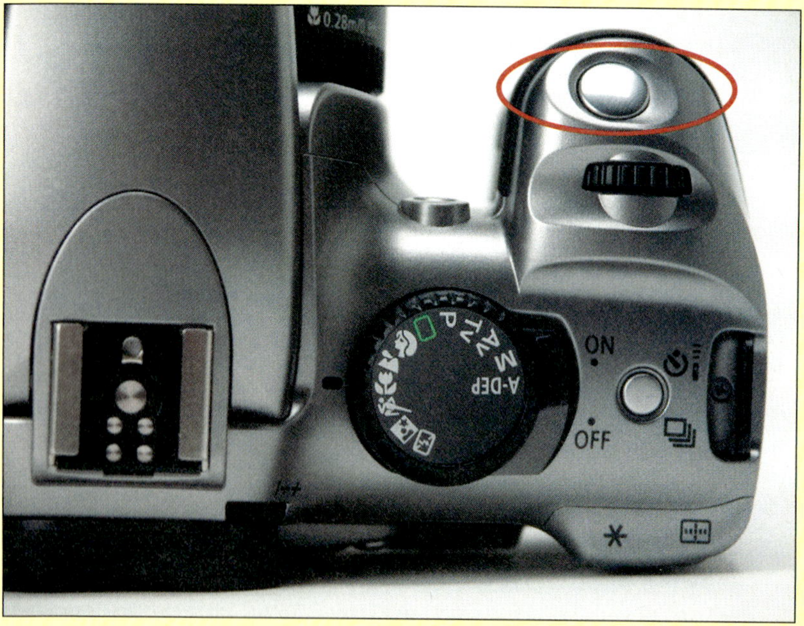

To take a shot with the Digital Rebel, it's pretty much like any other camera—just press the Shutter release button on the top right front of the camera (as shown here). Okay, things get a bit more complicated from here.

Focusing the viewfinder eyepiece

> *This helps make sure you can see the focus clearly*

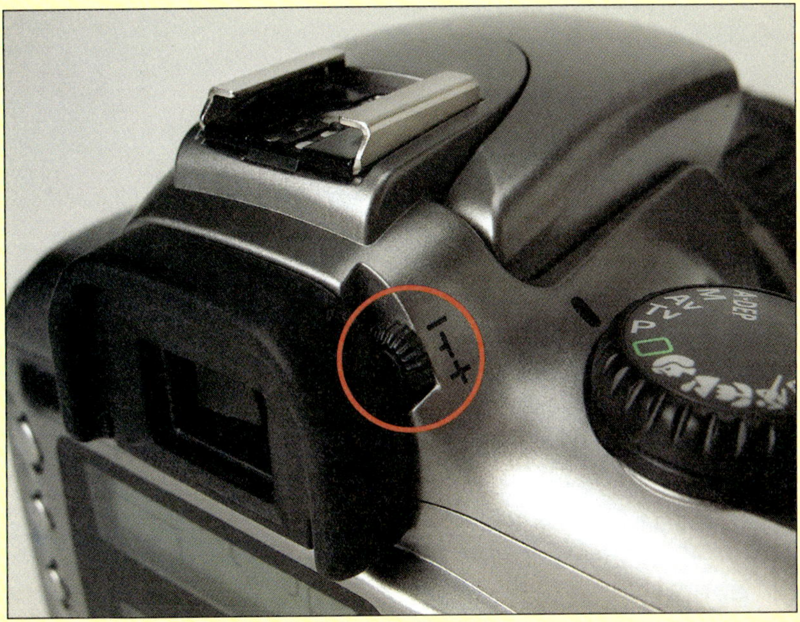

There's an adjustment on the Rebel's eyepiece that lets you adjust for variations among different people's vision—enabling you to see more clearly through the eyepiece (which is critical to making sure the images you shoot are indeed in focus). This setting (called the Dioptric Adjustment Knob) is found just to the left of the eyepiece (as shown above). Look through the viewfinder and then move the knob until you get the clearest possible image for your particular vision.

Using the autofocus

> This is done through a seven-point grid in the viewfinder

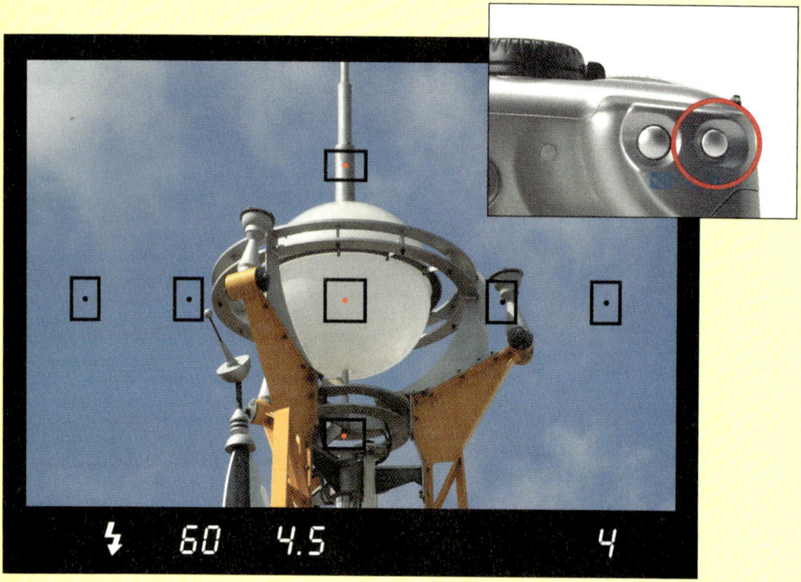

The Rebel's autofocus system uses seven focus points (tiny boxes), which appear in the center of the viewfinder. When one or more of those seven points focuses on an object, a red light appears in the center of each box, letting you know it's focused on the object seen behind the red dot. If you want the autofocus to focus on the center point, but the red square appears focused on the far-left box, you can make the focus jump to the center by simply moving the camera until the center point is on the subject, then pressing the Shutter button halfway down to lock the focus on the center point. Another way is to hold down the AF (autofocus) Selector button (it's on the back of the camera, and is shown circled in the inset photo above) and turn the Main Dial (the round knob on top of the camera, right behind the Shutter button) until the focus point you want turns red.

Locking in your focal point using autofocus

> *Just press down the Shutter button halfway down*

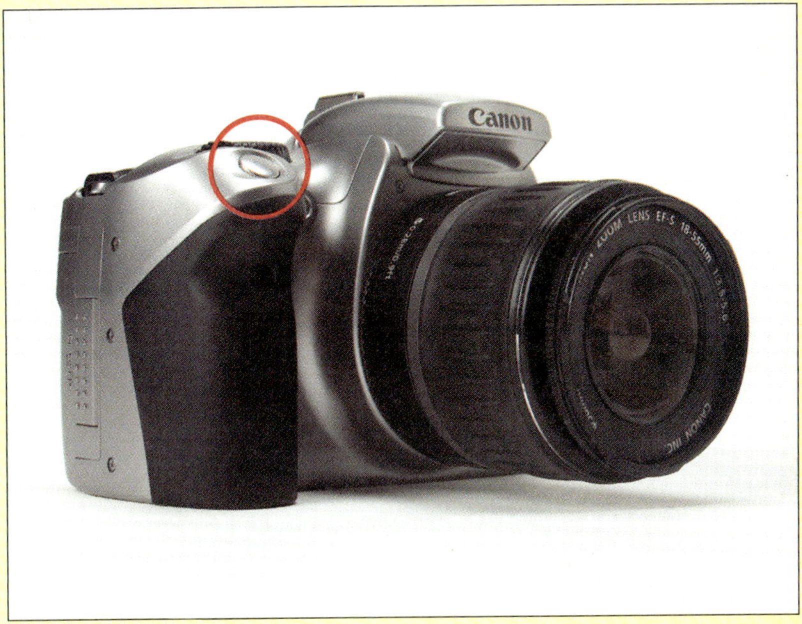

The Digital Rebel has a fantastic autofocus feature, but it's not clairvoyant—as you move the camera, and as objects that you're shooting move, the autofocus is constantly changing what it's focusing on. When it does focus on your intended object, gently press the Shutter button down halfway to lock the autofocus on target. As long as the Shutter button (circled above) is pressed halfway down, the autofocus won't refocus on anything else. Then, when you're ready, just press the Shutter button all the way down to take your shot. So in short, press the Shutter button halfway down, let the autofocus lock on, then shoot!

How to tell if your autofocus is locked on

> Look in the viewfinder

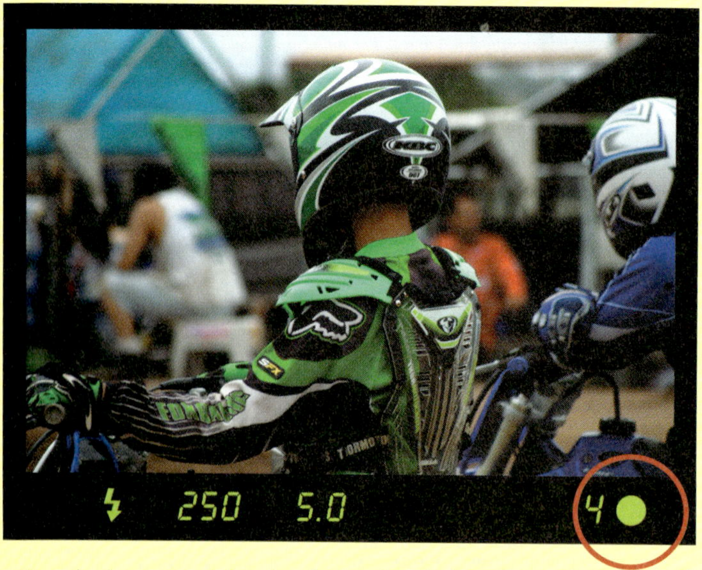

At the bottom of the viewfinder, just below the viewing area, is a row of indicators. If you see a solid green dot on the right side (as shown above), that's the Focus Confirmation Light telling you that your focus is locked on (you must first hold down the Shutter button halfway to see the Focus Confirmation Light). By the way, the number that appears immediately to the left of that light tells you how many continuous shots you can shoot in one burst by pressing and holding the Shutter button all the way down.

Turning off autofocus

> *You do this on the lens itself, not on the camera body*

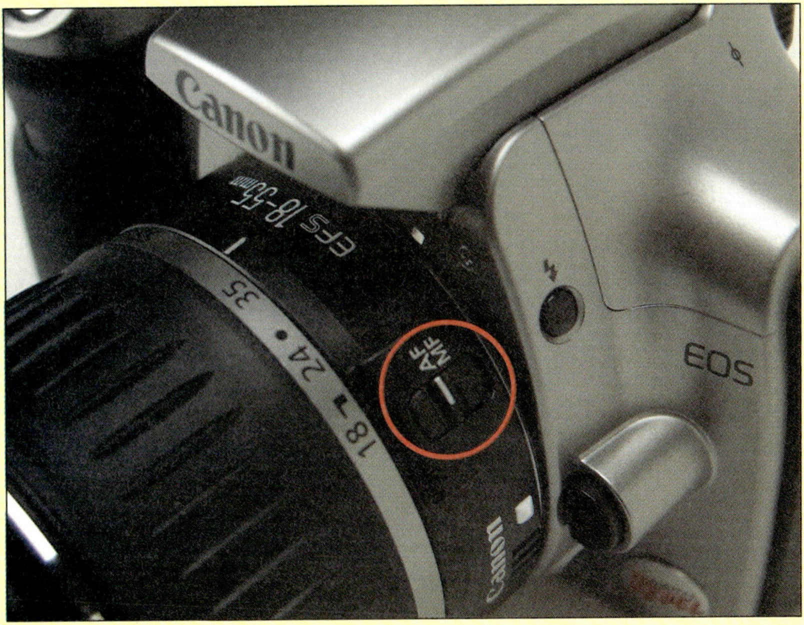

By default, your lens is set to autofocus (which is really incredibly handy and I recommend it highly). But if you'd prefer to manually focus the lens, surprisingly, the control to do this isn't on the camera, but on the lens itself. If you look at the lens, you'll see a small switch with AF on one end and MF on the other. Move the toggle switch on the lens from AF (autofocus) to MF (manual focus). Now you can focus the lens manually using the focus ring on the lens itself.

Using the built-in flash

> *If the Rebel thinks you need a flash, you're gettin' a flash*

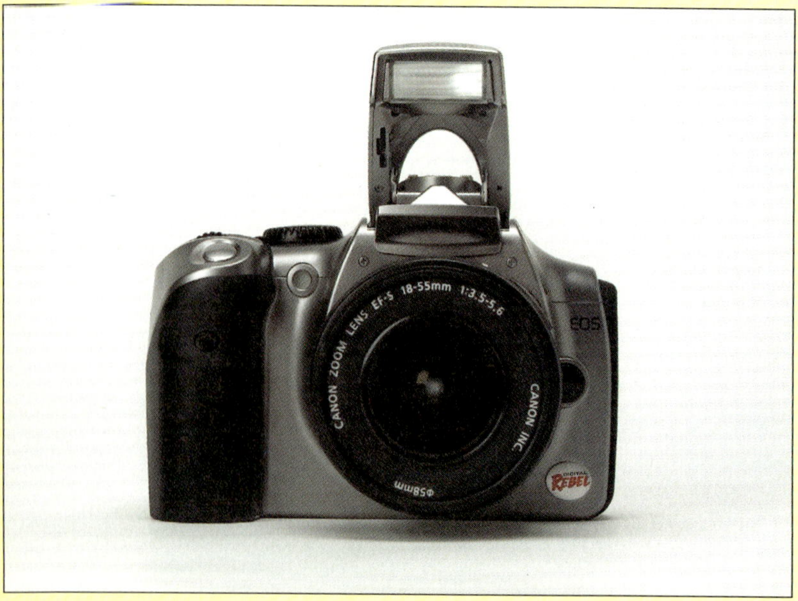

When you're shooting in Full Auto, Portrait, Night Portrait, or Close Up mode, the Rebel automatically senses if there's not enough light to properly expose the photo. So it pops up and turns on the built-in flash for you.

How to tell if your flash is ready to fire

> *The indicator is found in the viewfinder*

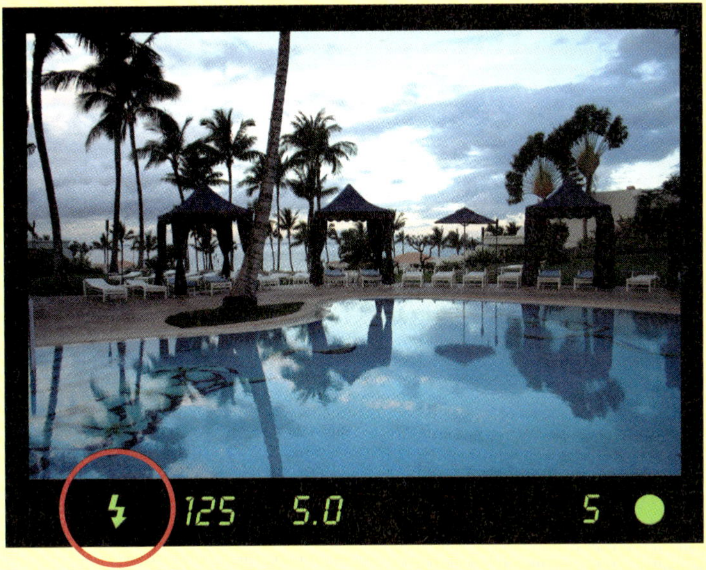

If you look in the viewfinder (when the camera is turned on, of course) you'll see some symbols and numbers displayed below the viewing area. If you see a lightning bolt icon on the left side, it means the flash is ready to fire. If the flash is up and you don't see that bolt, it means the flash is still charging, so don't shoot until you see the bolt.

How to reduce "red eye"

> *You're one button away from ridding yourself of this curse*

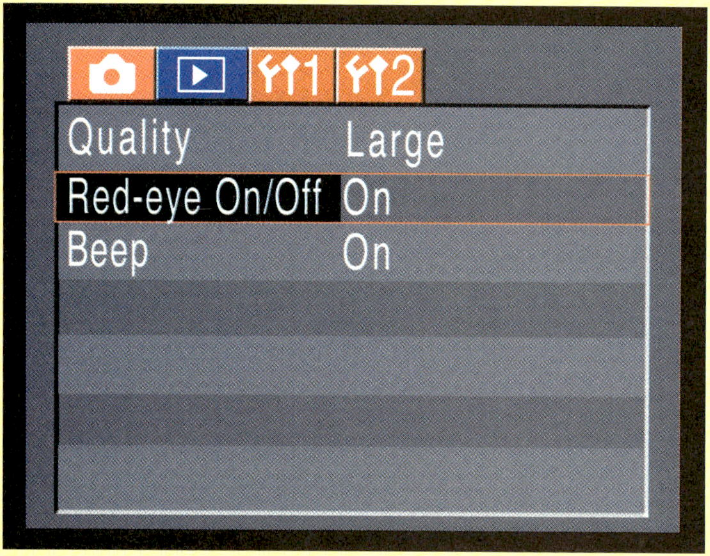

Digital cameras are notorious for producing photos where the subjects have "red eye." This is partly because the flash on digital cameras is mounted right above the lens, but it also has to do with how the eye's pupil reacts to a bright flash in a dark room. The pop-up flash on the Rebel pops up fairly high, away from the lens, so that helps alleviate some red eye, but sadly it doesn't stop it all. You can get rid of most of it, however, by turning on Red Eye Reduction. Here's how: Press the Menu button on the back of the camera, then use the down arrow button to scroll down to Red Eye and press the Set button to turn it on. Now, when you hold the Shutter button halfway down, a tiny light located to the right of the lens will flash (called a preflash), and that contracts your subject's pupils a moment before the real flash fires, reducing red eye.

Shooting without the flash

> *What if you don't want flash, but the Auto modes think you do?*

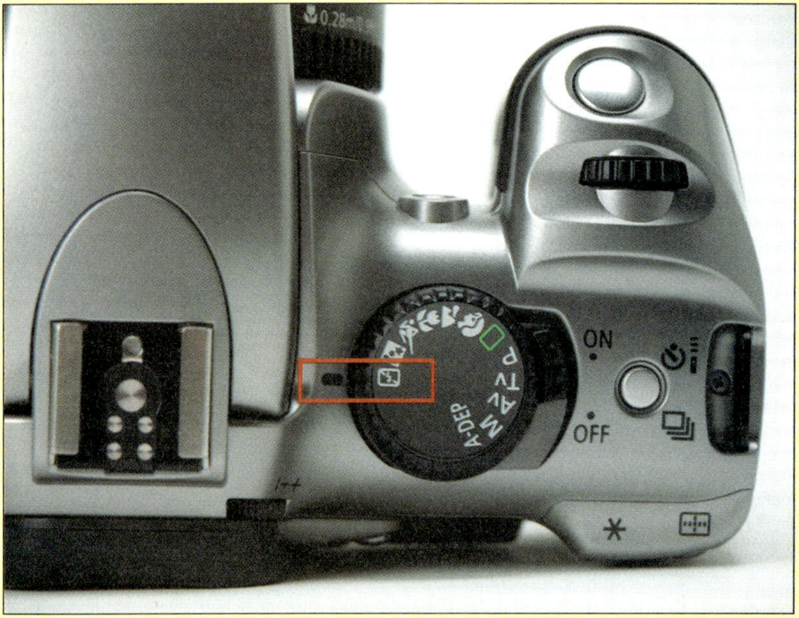

If you want to use an Auto mode (so the exposure, shutter speed, etc., are all set for you), but you don't want the built-in flash to pop up, there is a special No Flash mode for just that purpose. You choose No Flash from the Mode Dial (the icon is a rectangle with a lightning bolt inside it, and with the international symbol for "NO!" over the bolt). Since that's such a lame description of the icon, perhaps I should just say it's the last Auto mode on the dial. That's easier, eh?

Turning the flash on/off in manual modes

> *The key word here is manual, you're doing the work*

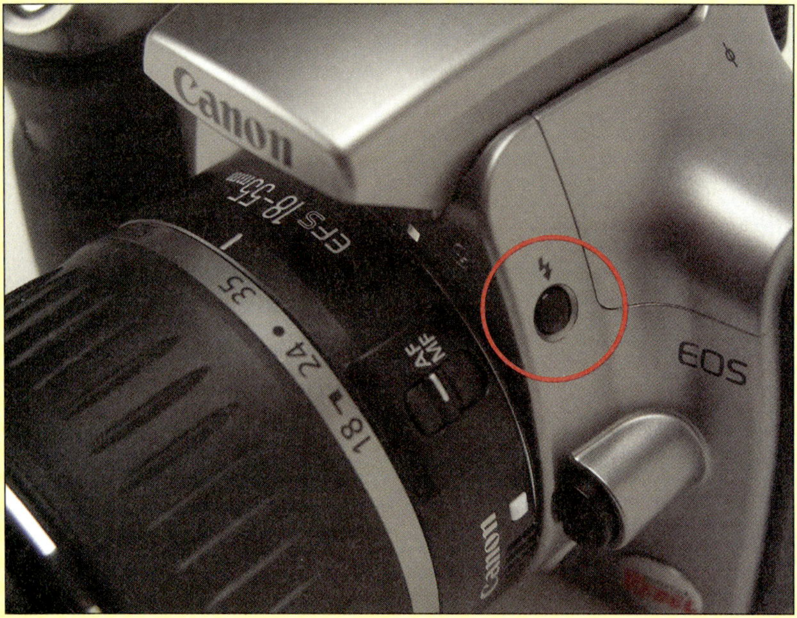

If you're not shooting in one of the Rebel's Auto modes, then turning on the flash (or turning it off) is entirely up to you. So if you're working in one of the camera's Creative modes (like A-DEP, M, Av, Tv, or P) and you want to have the built-in flash pop up, you must press the Flash button, which is found on the front side of the camera—it's a small, round black button just to the left of the front of the flash (as shown above). Press that button (the one with a lightning bolt icon above it) and the built-in flash pops up. If you decide you no longer want flash, you have to push the pop-up flash unit down until it clicks back into position. I know—it sounds so "manual" (and it is!).

Shooting in Full Auto mode

> *This way the camera does all the work—you just point and shoot*

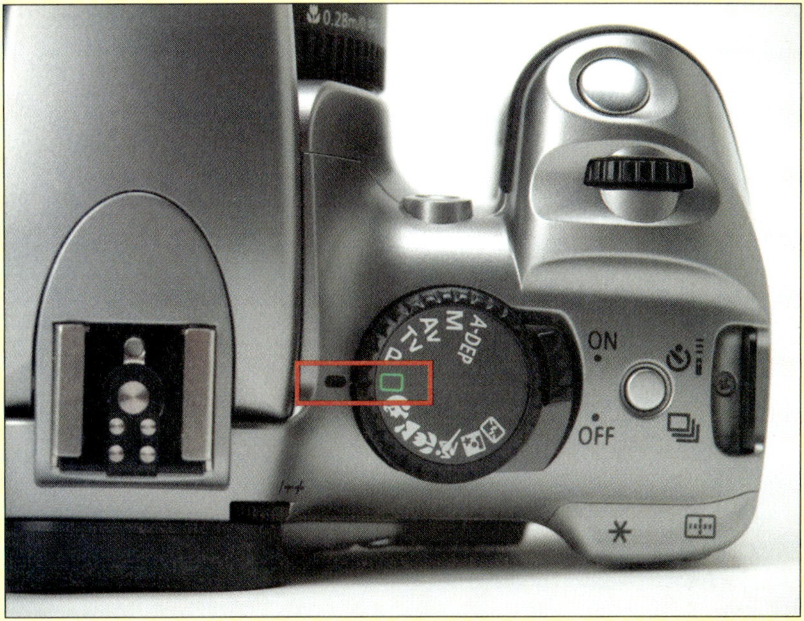

Most people using the Rebel (with the exception of professionals and really fussy high-end amateurs) use the camera in Full Auto mode, meaning the camera does all the dirty work for you—it focuses, sets the exposure, picks the right shutter speed, etc. Basically, all you have to do is point and shoot. I know plenty of people who have never used any other mode than this, and yet they've gone on to live happy and productive lives. So if ease of use is important to you, you'll want to get to know Full Auto mode. To use it, just set the Mode Dial (on the top right of your camera) to the green square. That's it—you're in Full Auto. Fire away!

The setup for shooting great shots at night

> *Get a tripod, then change the Mode Dial. It's as simple as that.*

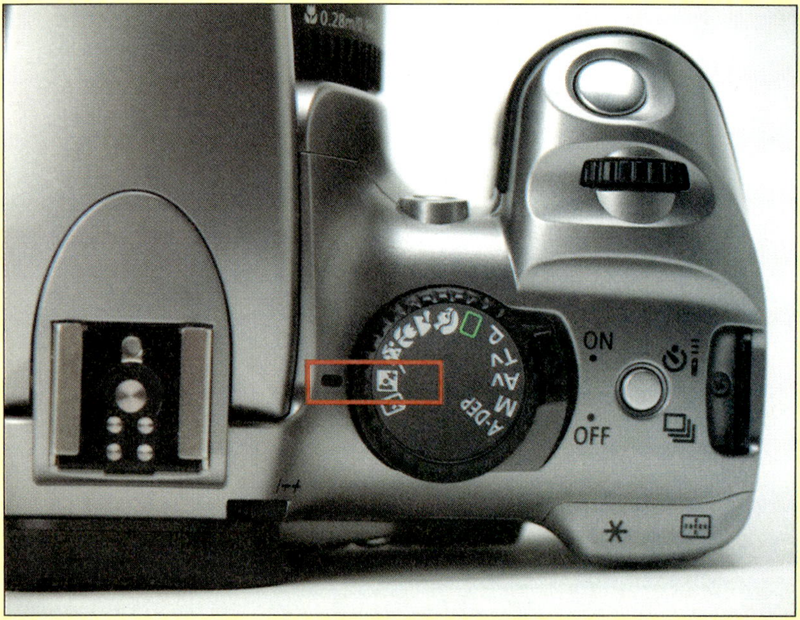

Getting great shots in low light is tough, because low-lighting situations require the Shutter to remain open longer, and therefore any minor movement on your part makes the photo incredibly blurry. To get around this, just do two things: (1) Use a tripod for low-light or night shots (you can buy one for a very reasonable price), and (2) set the Mode Dial on the top of your camera to Night Portrait mode (as shown above). Do these two things. You'll be amazed at the photos the Rebel will produce at night or in low-light situations.

How to set the camera for action shots

> *When things start moving, you need to adjust one setting*

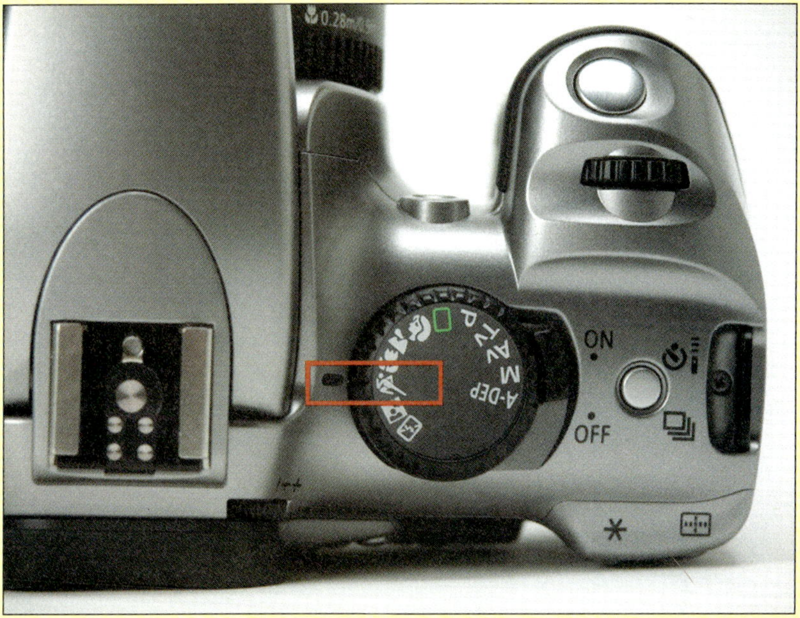

When you're shooting action shots (your kid's little league or soccer match, a pro sporting event, racing, skiing, people running, etc.), changing just one dial setting can make all the difference in the world. Just change the Mode Dial (at the top right of the camera) to Sports mode (the icon looks like the Olympic symbol for running, as shown above). This increases the shutter speed for you, and prevents blurry shots by basically stopping the motion. So if you're shooting action, and you want sharp photos, change that dial. It's a little thing that makes a huge difference.

How to shoot professional looking portraits

>The secret is depth of field, and you can get it with just one change

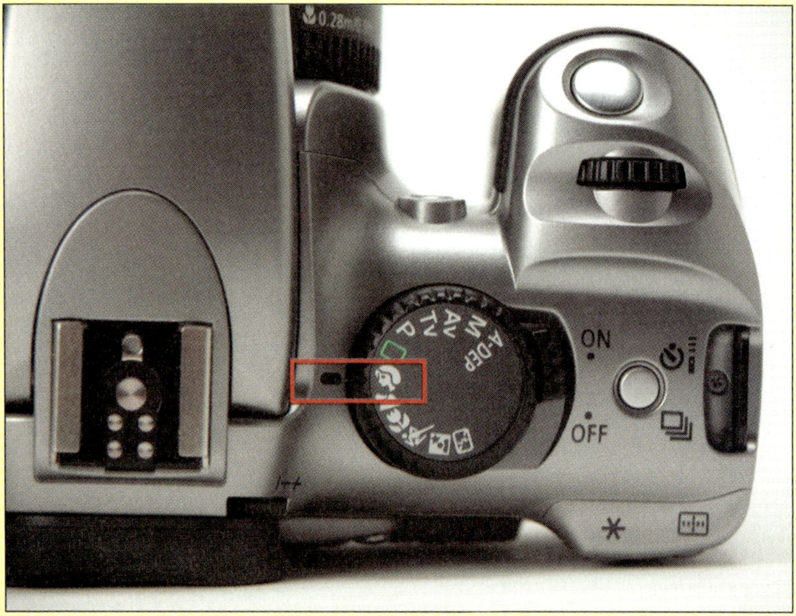

A popular trick used by professional portrait photographers is to use a shallow *depth of field*. What that means is that the person in the foreground of the portrait is sharply in focus, but the background is blurry and out of focus. This makes the subject stand out; it's especially useful when you're not shooting in a studio (you're shooting outdoors, on location, on vacation, etc.). To get this effect, just change the Mode Dial to Portrait (the icon looks like a woman's head facing left, as shown above). Now when you focus on the subject, the background will be blurry and out of focus.

How to shoot objects up close

> *It's not macro photography, but it's the next best thing*

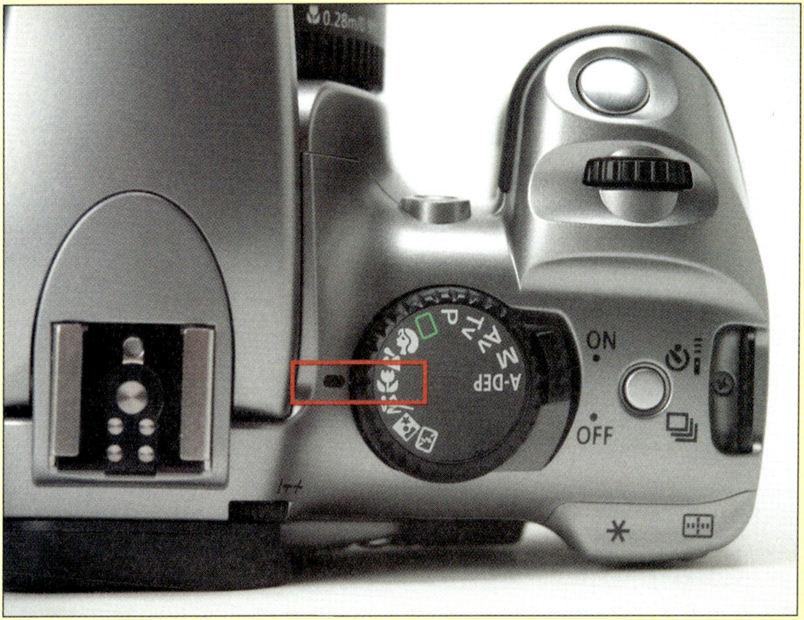

If you're shooting objects up close (like a close-up shot of a bee landing on a flower), there's a special mode that will help you get the best, sharpest shot possible. Just change the Mode Dial to Close-Up mode (the icon looks like a flower). This mode adds additional exposure metering, which helps you maintain sharpness and detail when focusing on close-up objects.

How to shoot landscapes

> *Shooting the great outdoors? Here's how to capture more of it.*

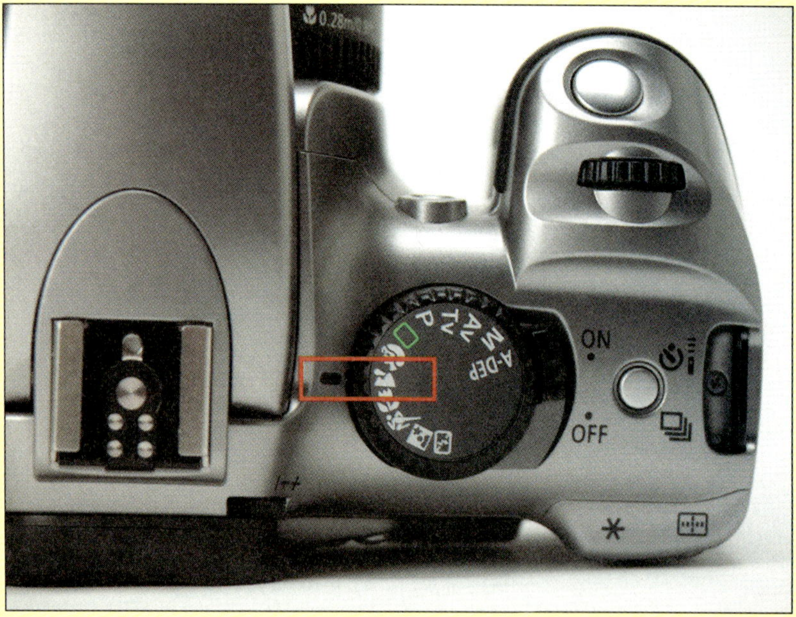

Although we love that shallow depth of field when we're shooting portraits, with landscapes we want to capture as much depth and as wide a field of focus as we can. That's precisely why there's a special mode just for shooting landscapes, called (are you ready for this?) Landscape mode. You get to it by turning the Mode Dial to Landscape (the icon for it looks like mountains, as shown above).

Using a zoom lens

> *How to zoom in tight, and zoom out for a wider view*

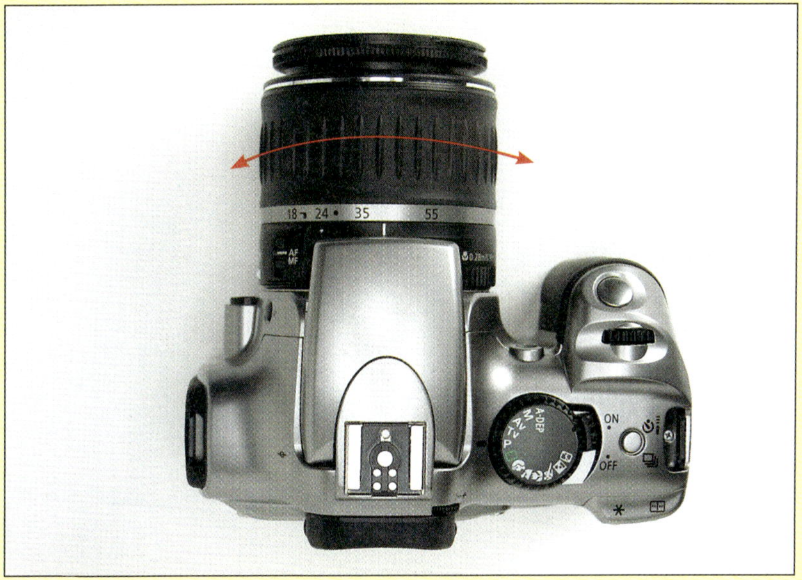

If you have a zoom lens with your Canon Digital Rebel (and if you bought the standard configuration, chances are you have at least an 18–55mm zoom lens), you can zoom just like you would with a traditional SLR—you rotate the barrel around the lens itself, not by pushing buttons on the camera.

Turning off Auto White Balance (AWB)

> *How to switch to manual white balance, should you need to*

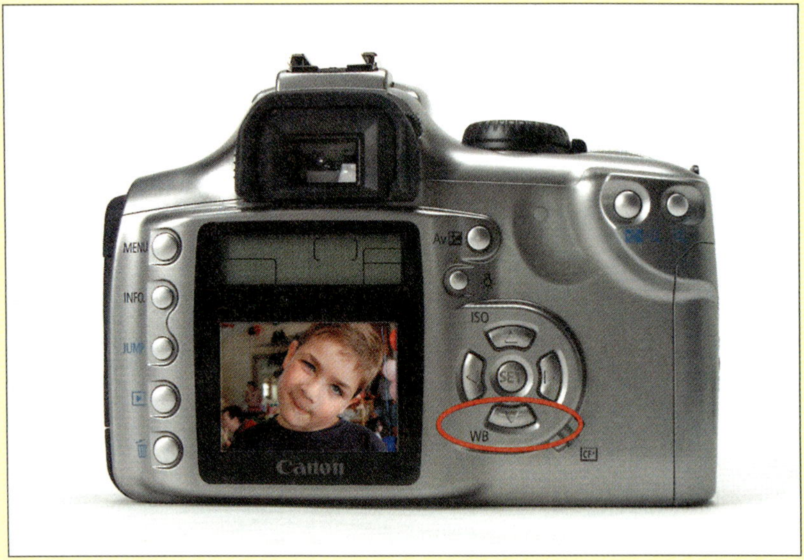

In the Auto modes the Rebel sets the white balance for you, automatically adjusting to different lighting conditions. However, if you feel the need to set the white balance manually, you can; but you can only do this when you're not shooting in an Auto mode. You have to be shooting in what Canon calls the "Creative modes," where basically you're on your own. So as long as your Mode Dial is set to either A-DEP, M, Av, Tv, or P you can adjust white balance yourself by simply pushing the bottom arrow button on the back of the camera (it says WB, for white balance and it's circled above). Start rotating the Main Dial (the one right behind the Shutter button), then look at the bottom left-hand corner of the LCD readout on the back of the camera, and you'll see the icons appear for the different white balance options, including Daylight, Shade, Cloudy, Flash, Fluorescent, and Tungsten.

How to tell how much battery time is left

> *Just take a look at the LCD info panel*

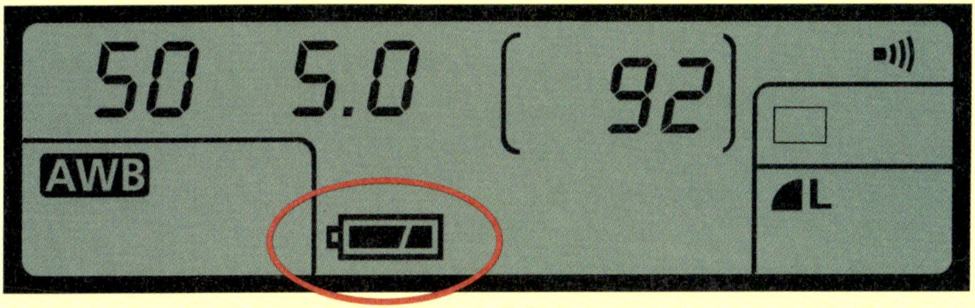

Want to know how much battery life you have on the current charge? Just make sure the camera's turned on, then look at the LCD info panel on the back of the camera (right above the preview window). At the bottom center (OK, it's a little offset to the left) is a battery charge indictor that looks like a battery. If the battery looks solid (filled with black) you've got a full change. If it looks half full, it's half full. If it's blinking, it's time to recharge, and fast!

Finding out how many shots you have left

> *This is one incredibly important number, and it's found on the LCD info panel*

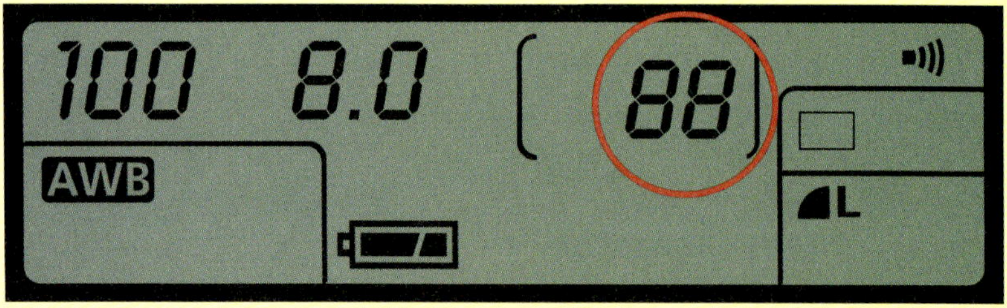

Because we're shooting digital and we don't have to keep popping in a new roll every 24 or 36 shots, we sometimes forget that memory cards do get full. So, want to know how many shots you have left on your memory card? Just turn the camera on and look at the LCD info panel above the color LCD monitor. See that number inside the brackets? That's how many shots you have left. If it's a big number, keep on shooting. If not, either delete some marginal-looking photos to make more room, or pop in another memory card with some room on it.

How to choose your image size settings

> *The smaller the image, the smaller the file size*

Format	Dimensions	Number of Shots
JPEG Large (Fine)	3072 x 2048 pixels	105 on 256 MB card
JPEG Large (Normal)	3072 x 2048 pixels	160 on 256 MB card
JPEG Medium (Fine)	2048 x 1360 pixels	180 on 256 MB card
JPEG Medium (Normal)	2048 x 1360 pixels	300 on 256 MB card
JPEG Small (Fine)	1536 x 1024 pixels	256 on 256 MB card
JPEG Small (Normal)	1536 x 1024 pixels	432 on 256 MB card
RAW	3072 x 2048 pixels	44 on 256 MB card

The Rebel offers four main size formats: JPEG Large (which creates files that are 3072 x 2048 pixels in size), JPEG Medium (2048 x 1360), JPEG Small (1536 x 1024), and RAW (this creates files that are 3072 x 2048, but because it's also the highest-quality format, it creates very large file sizes, so you get to shoot fewer photos per memory card). If you're going to output your photo in large sizes (like 8 x 10″ or above), you want to shoot in JPEG Large format. If you're only going to output 4 x 6″ prints, you can get away with JPEG Medium or perhaps even JPEG Small. RAW is a format used primarily by professionals who will edit the RAW photo with image-editing software like Adobe Photoshop CS.

How to choose your image-quality settings

> Each JPEG format has two different quality choices

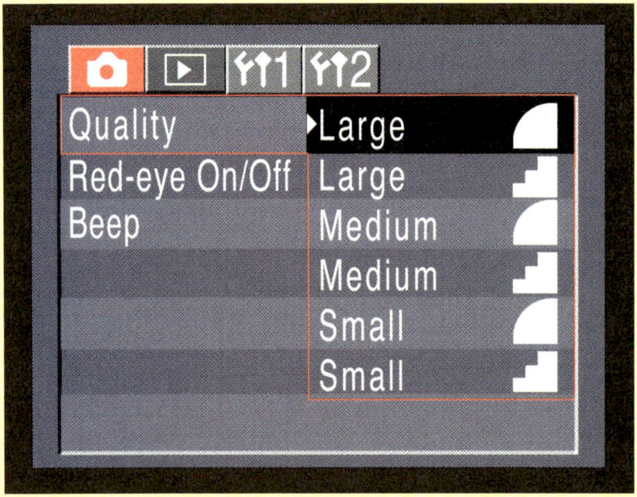

Each of the Rebel's quality settings (Large, Medium, and Small) offers two different quality settings: Fine and Normal. If you're shooting shots you care about (your children, portfolio shots, artistic shots, etc.), choose the Fine version of JPEG Large, Medium, or Small (it's the first of each of the two sizes in the list—so if you wanted to choose Fine, you'd pick the first "Large" in the list shown above). If you're shooting shots where the image quality isn't that important, use Normal quality (the second Large, Medium, or Small on the list), which creates more highly compressed photos with less quality but a smaller file size, so you can shoot more images on the same memory card. I generally recommend shooting JPEG Large for most instances. So where do you choose your quality settings? Press the Menu button on the top left of the camera, then press the Set button. This highlights the Quality menu on the color LCD monitor. Press the Set button, and the list of quality settings appears (shown above). Use the down arrow button to scroll to your choice, then press Set.

How to choose RAW format

> Choosing it is easy, but you can't choose it if you're shooting in an Auto mode

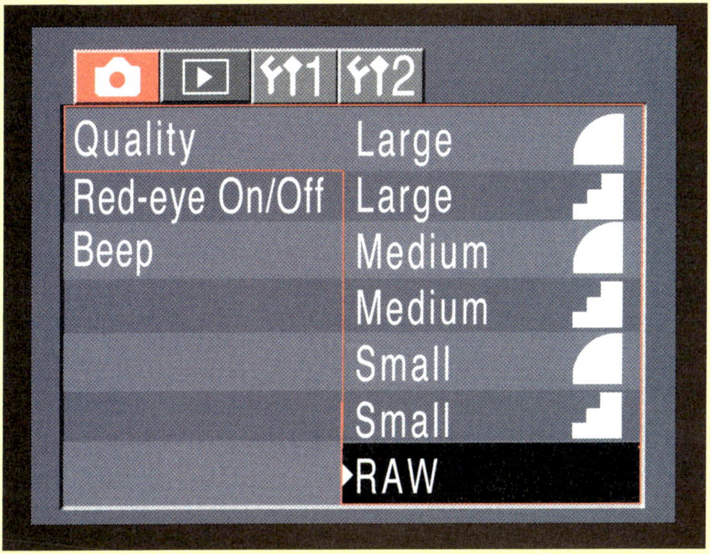

If you're looking to shoot in RAW format (the highest quality setting, primarily used by professionals), then chances are you're not shooting in one of the Auto modes, which is good because you can't choose RAW as a quality setting in any of the Auto modes. To choose RAW you must first be using one of the Creative modes—where you make most decisions yourself. Once you've switched the Mode Dial to either A-DEP, M, Av, Tv, or P, then press the Menu button on the top left rear of the camera and press the Set button. Press the Set button once again to see the list of Quality settings and at the very bottom is RAW (as shown above). Use the down arrow button to scroll down to RAW, then press the Set button. You're now shooting in RAW format.

How to know which quality format you are using

> *It's a code found on the LCD info panel*

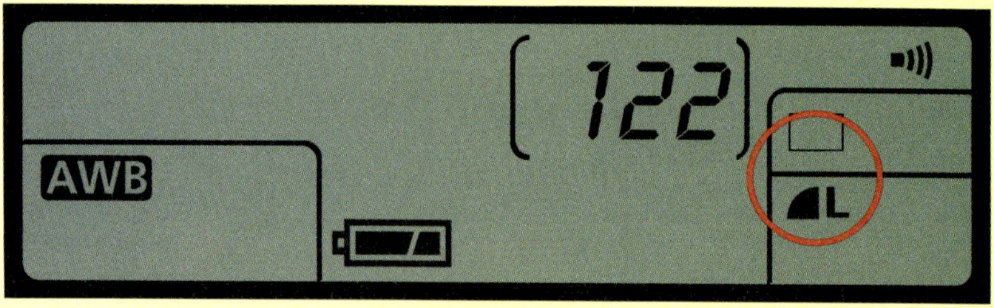

To quickly find out which size and quality format you're currently shooting in, look at the LCD info panel on the back of the camera, right above the color LCD monitor. Look in the bottom right-hand corner of the panel. If you're using Large JPEG Fine, you'll see a bold capital *L* and a rounded pie-wedge–shaped icon directly beneath it. If you're using JPEG Normal, the pie shape will look stair-stepped, rather than smooth, and the *L* will appear to the upper right of the stair-stepped icon. For the other two settings, for Medium you'll see an *M* and for Small an *S* (and the pie-shaped icons will be there as well). If you're shooting in RAW, the highest-quality format, you'll see the word RAW.

Seeing the LCD info panel in low-light situations

> *Luckily, it has its own light. You just have to know where it is.*

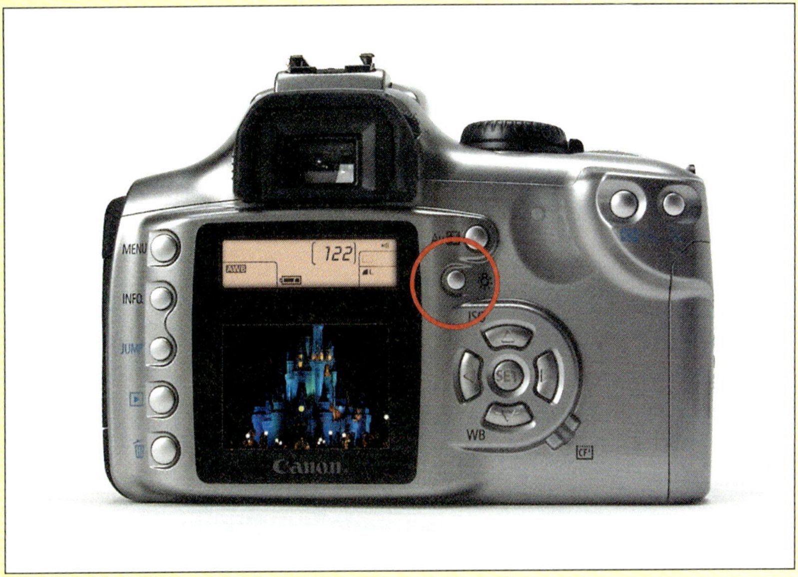

If you're in a situation where you can't clearly see the LCD info panel (you're shooting at night, say), there's a small light that will come on for a few seconds that illuminates just that area. It's found just to the right of the LCD panel itself, right above the letters *ISO*, and it has a light bulb icon to the right of it (as shown above). Press it and a backlight will come on to temporarily light the panel.

Reviewing your photos on the color LCD monitor

> *Once you take a photo, it's displayed for your "instant review"*

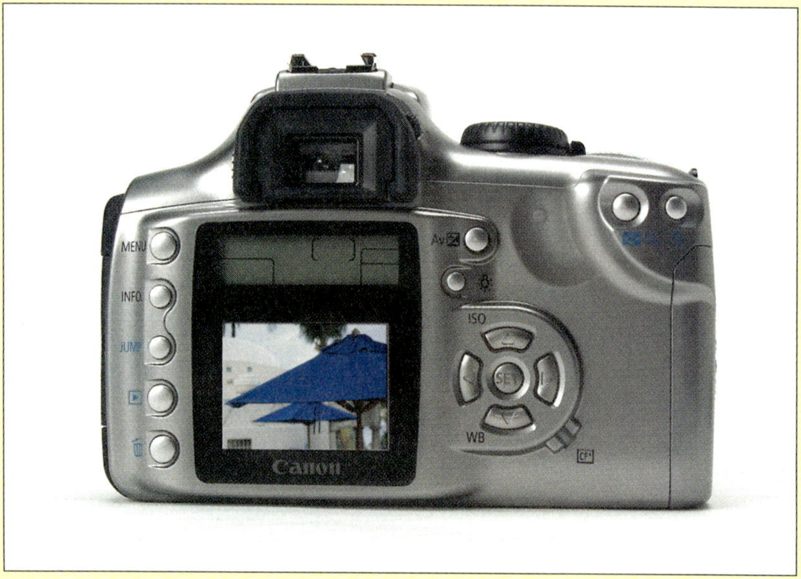

One of the coolest things about digital photography is that right after you press the Shutter button, a small color image of the shot you just took appears in the color LCD monitor on the back of the camera. This gives you a quick look to see if the photo was in focus, whether you moved the camera, whether the subject's eyes closed, etc. so you pretty much instantly know whether you need to take the shot again.

How to zoom in on your preview photo

> *You can zoom in and see if the subject is really in focus*

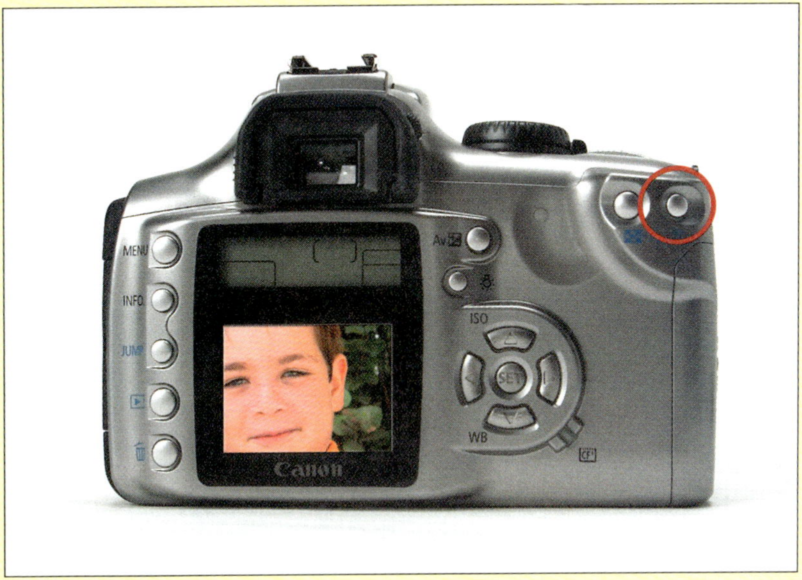

Judging whether or not a photo is in sharp focus is sometimes hard to do using the tiny color LCD monitor on the back of the camera, but luckily you can zoom in on your preview to get a nice close look. Just press the Magnify plus button (located on the back top right of the camera) to zoom in on the preview, and press the minus button on the left to zoom back out. While zoomed in, if you need to move around the photo just use the arrow buttons on the back of the camera.

How to keep your preview photo on screen longer

> *By default, it goes away in 2 seconds, but you can change that*

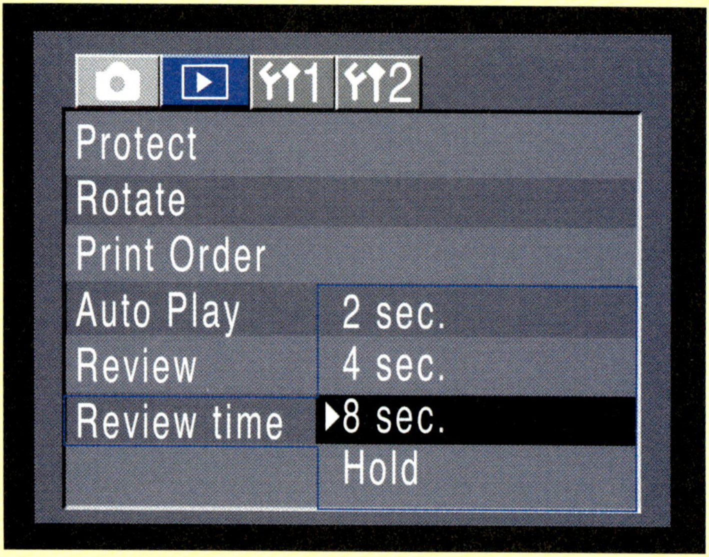

Although you get an instant preview of the photo you just took (called a "review"), by default it stays up there for only 2 seconds. However, you can have it stay up there longer (up to 8 seconds) by pressing the Menu button on the top right back of the camera, then press the right arrow button once to scroll over to the Playback menu. Press the Set button then use the down arrow button to scroll down to "Review time." Press the Set button again and a list will appear (shown above) where you can choose how many seconds you'd like to review the shot you just took. Simply highlight the amount of review time you want, and press the Set button to lock it in.

How to jump 10 photos forward/backward

> *It makes getting to the photos your looking for much faster*

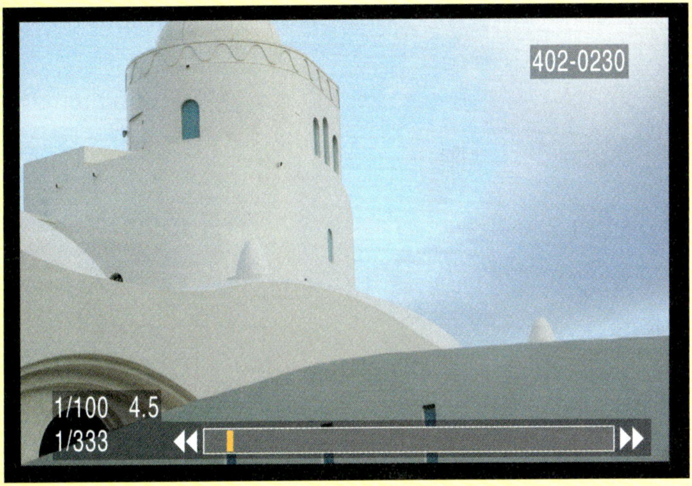

Let's say you have 300 or more photos on your memory card, and you're trying to quickly locate 10 or 12 shots that are somewhere on the card. Here's a quick way to find a certain set of shots without having to view all 300, one at a time. Start by pressing the Play button (so you can start reviewing your photos), then press the Jump button right above the Play button. This changes the right and left arrow buttons so that when you press either one, instead of moving through one photo at a time, it will now jump 10 photos at a time, letting you find what you're looking for about 10 times faster. Once you locate the set of photos you're looking for, press the Jump button again to return to searching one by one.

Getting info on your photos

> *How to display the background info for the image on the LCD monitor*

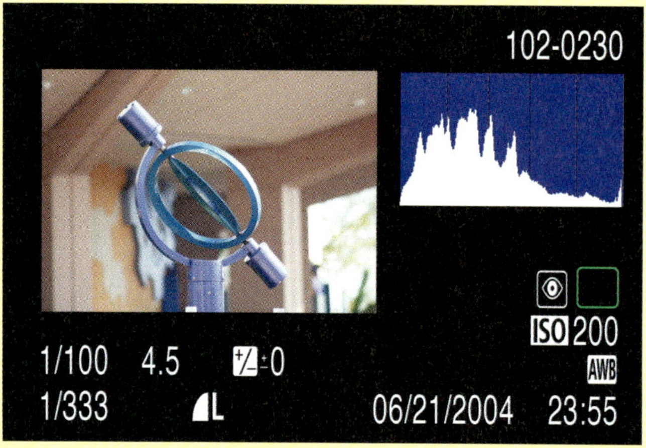

If you want to quickly find out the important background information on a photo you're reviewing on the color LCD monitor, just press the Info button on the back left side of the camera. This brings up an info window that shows a wide range of information, including the ISO for the shot, the shutter speed, the f-stop, the quality setting, and more. It also displays a histogram of the photo showing its tonal range displayed in a graph so you can see if the exposure is correct (that there is a full range of shadows, midtones, and highlights). To return to a regular preview, press the Info button again.

Rotate your vertical preview photos automatically

> *This keeps you from having to turn the camera sideways to see your preview*

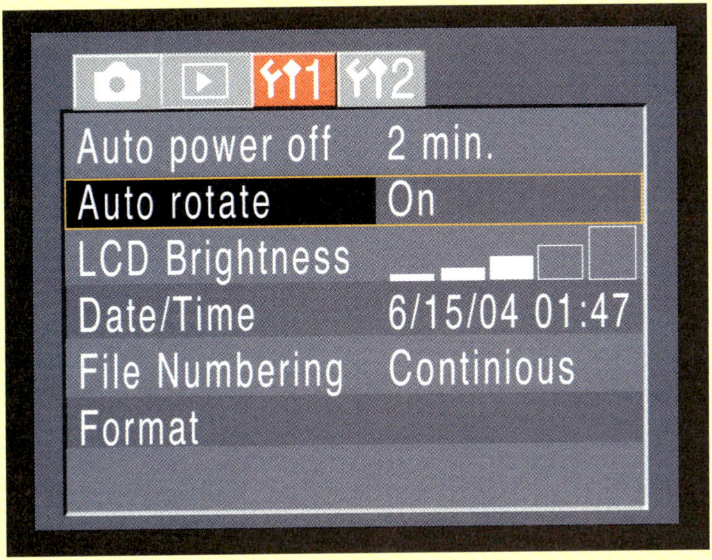

If you turn the camera vertically to take a photo in portrait orientation (meaning, if you turn the camera on its side to take a shot that's vertical instead of horizontal), this can create a problem when the photo is displayed in the color LCD monitor because it will be displayed on its side. But it doesn't have to be. You can have the Digital Rebel automatically rotate your vertical (portrait orientation) shots so they're facing upright. You do this by pressing the Menu button, the using the right arrow button on the back of the camera to scroll over to Set-up Menu 1. Press the Set button, then scroll down to "Auto rotate," then press the Set button again to turn it on.

Getting an index view of your preview photos

> *Here's how to quickly view nine tiny thumbnails of your photos*

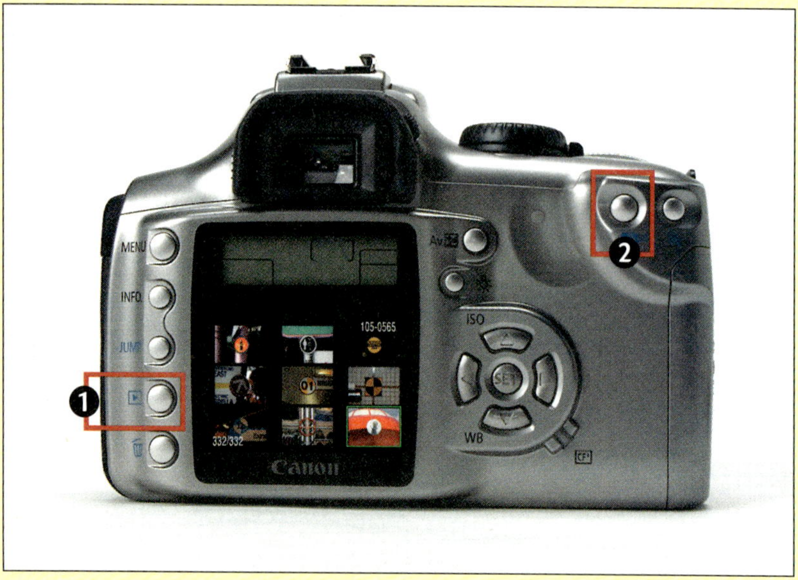

If you want to look at more than one photo at one time, just press the Play button (it's the second button from the bottom on the left rear of the camera [1]). Then press the Index button, which is located on the top right of the back of the camera (2), and your photos will be displayed nine at a time in Index mode on the color LCD monitor. To see more photo at this small nine-at-a-time index size, press the left and right arrow buttons. To see a particular index photo at full preview size, press your arrow buttons until a green border appears around the photo you want, then press the Play button on the back left side of the camera. You can also navigate using the Main Dial located just behind the Shutter button.

How to see a slide show of your photos

> *You can view it on the color LCD monitor on the back of your camera*

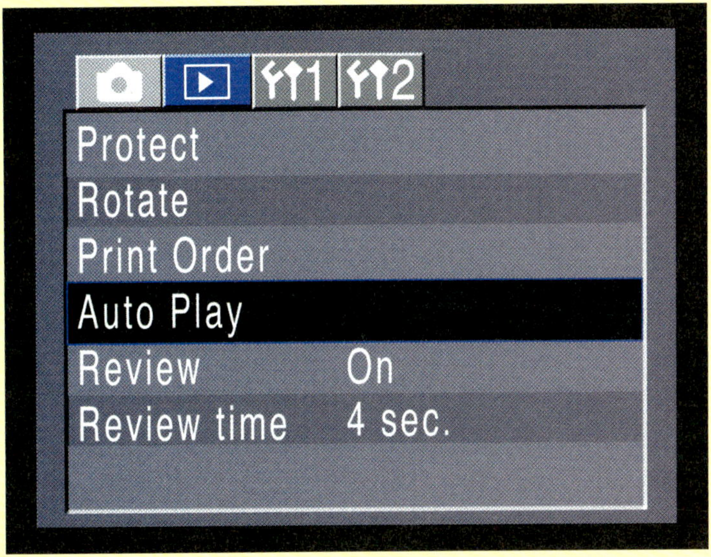

Anytime you'd like to see a slide show of the photos currently on your memory card, just press the Menu button on the back of the camera, the press the right arrow button once to scroll over to the Play menu, then press the Set key to enter that menu. Now press the down arrow button three times to scroll down to Auto Play (as shown above). Press the Set button and your slide show begins on the color LCD monitor on the back of the camera. To pause the slide show, press the Set button. To resume, press the Set button again. To stop the slide show, press the Menu button.

How to watch your slide show on your TV

> *Here's how to take your images to the big screen*

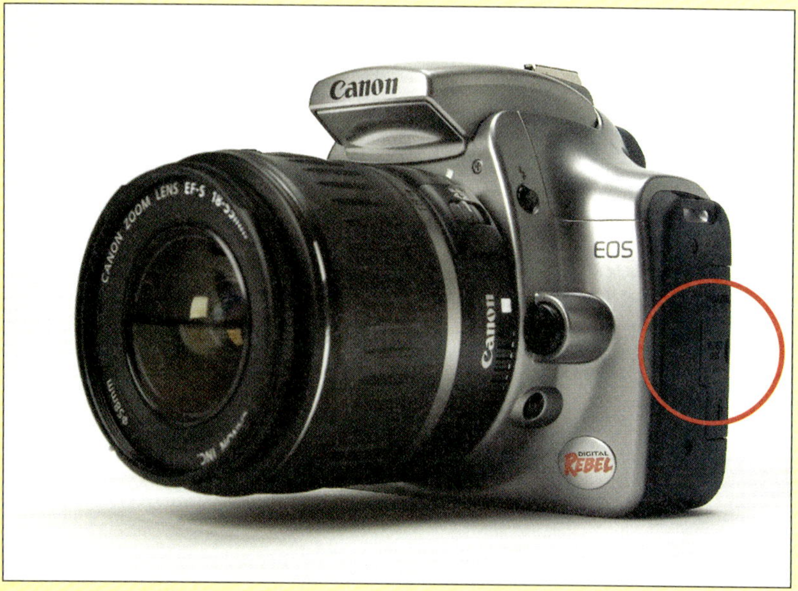

You've already learned how to view a "mini slide show" on the back of your camera, but if you're ready to see your images on a bigger screen, you can connect your Digital Rebel directly to your TV using the video-out jack on the side of your camera. Just pull open the rubber cover protecting the jacks (shown circled above), insert a video-out cable, and connect the cable to the inputs on the front of your television. Then press the Menu button on the back of the camera, press the right arrow button once to scroll over to the Play menu, then press the down arrow button four times to scroll down to Auto Play. Press the Set button, and the slide show begins. To pause it, press the Set button. To resume it, press the Set button. To stop, press the Menu button.

How to erase the photo you just took

> *Here's how to erase a bad shot*

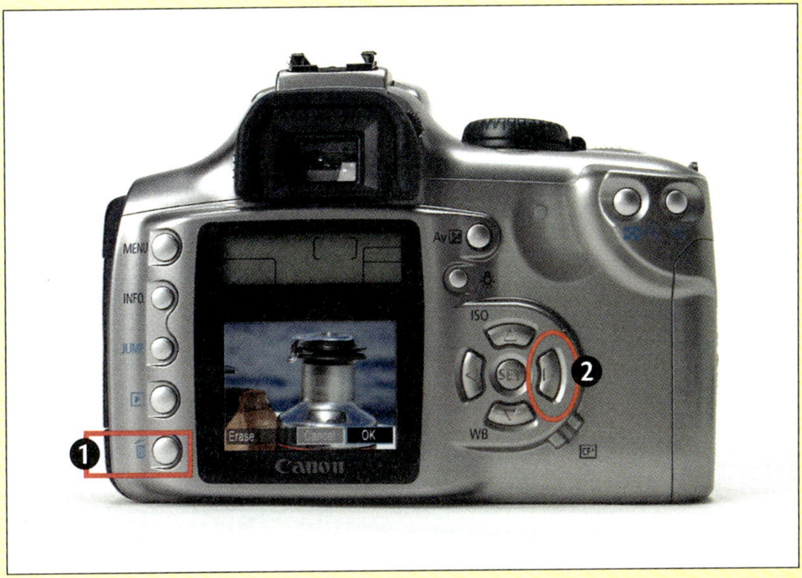

If you just took a photo, reviewed it, and decided it's not worth keeping, you can erase it by pressing the Trash button on the back bottom left side of your camera (it's in the red rectangle above). The word Erase will appear along the bottom of the photo in the color LCD monitor. Cancel is selected by default, so if you want to erase it, press the right arrow button (it has a red oval around it above) to move over to OK, and press the Set button. That's it—it's gone.

How to erase a photo from your memory card

> *Erasing photos you don't want frees up room for new photos*

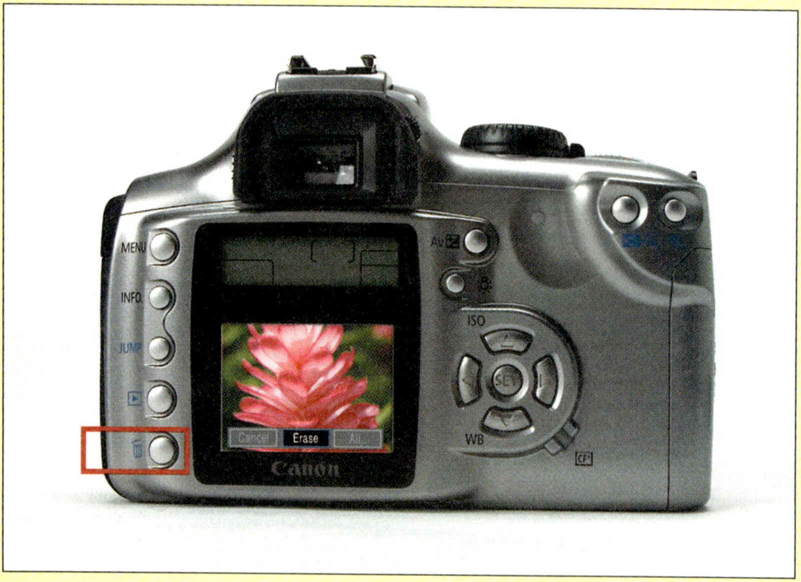

If you want to free up some space on your memory card by erasing photos you know you don't want to keep, first press the Play button on the back of the camera (it's the second button from the bottom on the left side of the camera). Then use the left and right arrow buttons to look through the images on your memory card. When you come to a photo you want to erase, press the Trash button (it's right below the Play button). This brings up a menu over the bottom of the photo in the LCD monitor. Cancel is chosen by default, so press the right arrow button once to toggle over to Erase, then press the Set button to actually erase that photo. Continue scrolling and erasing any other photos the same way.

How to protect a photo from being accidentally erased

> *If you've got a great shot, you might want to protect it*

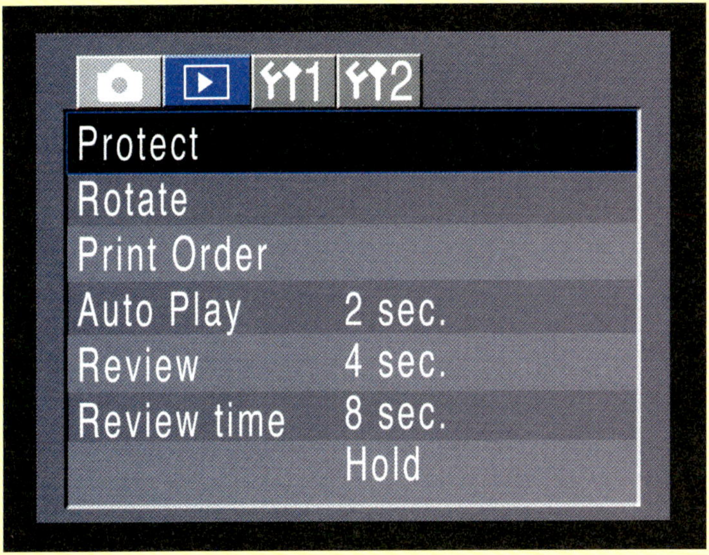

If you have a photo you want to keep from being accidentally erased, you can protect that photo by locking it. Once you use the Play button and the left/right arrow buttons to find the photo you want to protect, press the Menu button (on the back of the camera, top left), then press the right arrow button once to move to the Play menu. Press the down arrow button once to scroll down to Protect (as shown above), then press the Set button. This adds a tiny blue lock icon to the preview of your photo, letting you know this photo is protected from accidental erasure.

How to erase all your photos

> *Here's how to empty out your memory card*

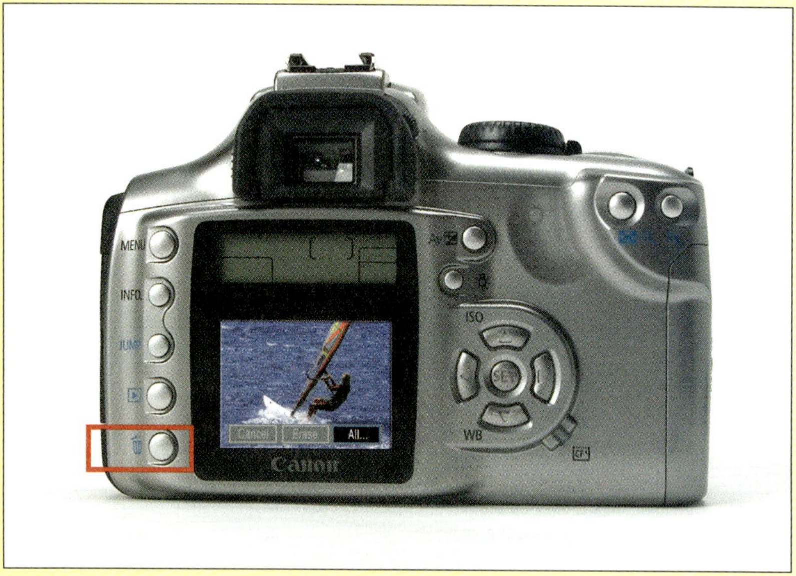

If you want to quickly erase all the photos on your memory card and start over with a blank card, just press the Play button on the back of your camera to enter Review mode, then press the Trash button on the bottom left rear of your camera. This adds a little Erase menu below your currently displayed image. To erase all the photos on your memory card, press the right arrow button twice to scroll over to "All" (as in "erase all my photos") then press the Set button. There is no "undo," so make darn sure you want to erase all your photos before you press the Set button to delete them all. Another way to erase all your photos is to format your memory card (as shown on page 5).

Getting photos onto your computer

> *How to move them from the camera to your computer for editing*

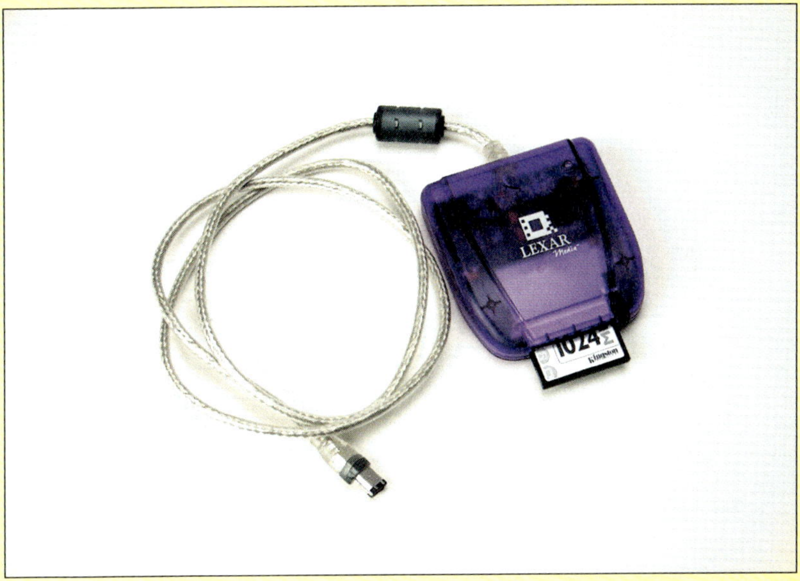

Although you might be tempted to connect the USB cable (included with your Digital Rebel) from your camera to your computer to download your photos, don't do it—it's unbearably slow. Instead, buy an inexpensive CompactFlash card reader (available at any consumer electronics store). Then eject your memory card from your camera: Slide open the memory compartment on the right side of your camera, and press the small black Eject button to pop your memory card out. Next, slide your card into the card reader, and plug the reader into your computer. This method will make downloading dramatically faster because it mounts your memory card on your computer's desktop as if it were another computer disk, so it transfers your photos in just a couple of minutes (instead of a couple of hours).

How to get more battery life

> *Here are the things to avoid that drain battery life*

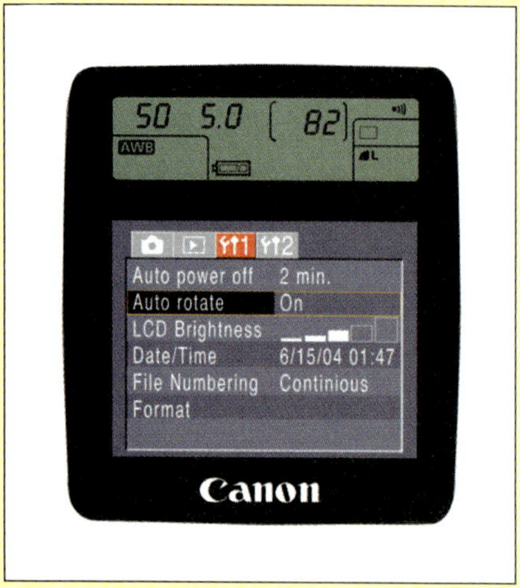

The single thing that probably drains the battery more than anything else is using the color LCD monitor on the back of the camera (shown above—it's the bottom screen). You're basically powering a small TV screen, so it eats up battery. Also, using the light for the LCD panel (shown above, it's the smaller, top screen) eats up a sizable amount of memory if you use it too often; so if you can avoid overusing either of these two (in particular the LCD monitor), you'll get longer battery life. That doesn't mean you shouldn't use these two features, but if you're getting low on battery juice, start using them sparingly.

Setting your "film" speed (ISO)

> *You can still choose a speed of 100, 200, 400, etc., and get equivalent results*

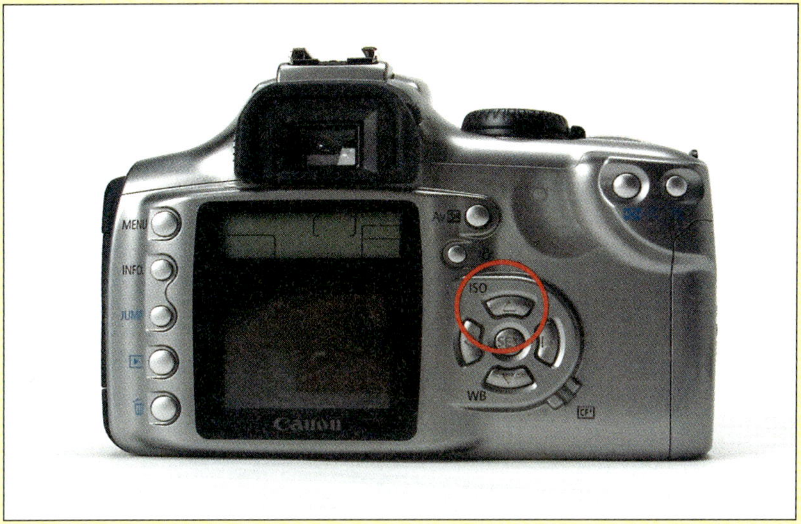

Back in the old days (when people actually bought film for traditional cameras), the first decision you had to make was what speed of film to choose (called ISO). You'd buy 100-speed film for shooting in direct sunlight or 400-speed for shooting at night or in low-light situations. Remember those days? Well, the Digital Rebel lets you do more than remember them, because you can set a digital equivalent of the film speed right on the camera, to approximate the effect of traditional film speed. To set the speed (your "digital ISO"), just press the up arrow button on the back of the camera (it says ISO just to the left of that button), then use the Main Dial (that's the black circular dial located directly behind the Shutter button) to choose your film speed, from 100 on up to 1600 (the ISO amount appears in the LCD info panel and in the viewfinder).

Running the camera in manual mode

> *What to do when you want to control everything yourself*

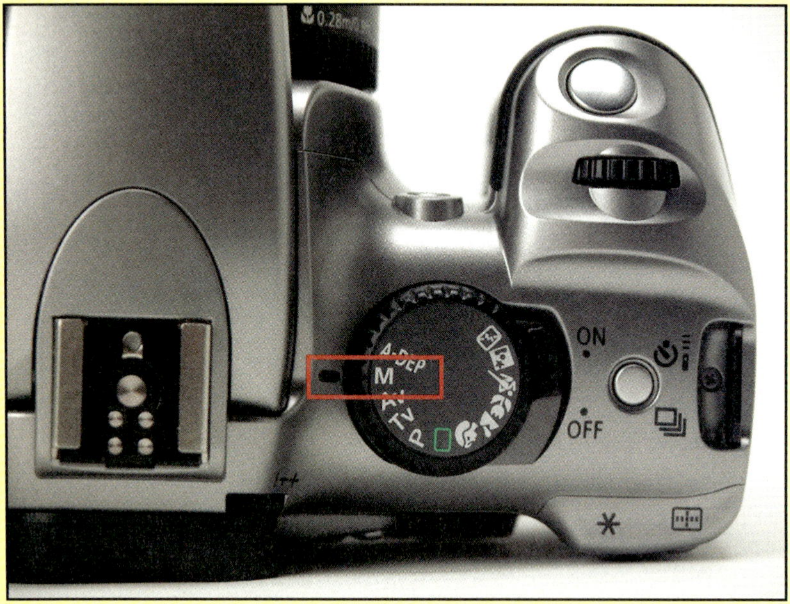

If you're one of those people who likes to do everything yourself, then you'll probably enjoy the Digital Rebel's manual mode, which lets you set the shutter speed and exposure manually. You enter this mode by changing the Mode Dial (at the top of the camera) to M (for Manual). While in this manual mode, you can set the shutter speed by moving the Main Dial (that's the circular dial right behind the Shutter release on the top of the camera). As you move it, the shutter speed will increase/decrease, and you can see the current setting by looking either on the LCD panel or in the viewfinder. You can also change the exposure manually by first holding the Av +/– button (that's the Aperture Value button located to the immediate right of the LCD panel) and then using the Main Dial again to change the f-stop settings, which will also be displayed in the LCD panel and viewfinder.

Restoring the camera's factory default settings

> *Want to start over, like you just opened the box? Here's how.*

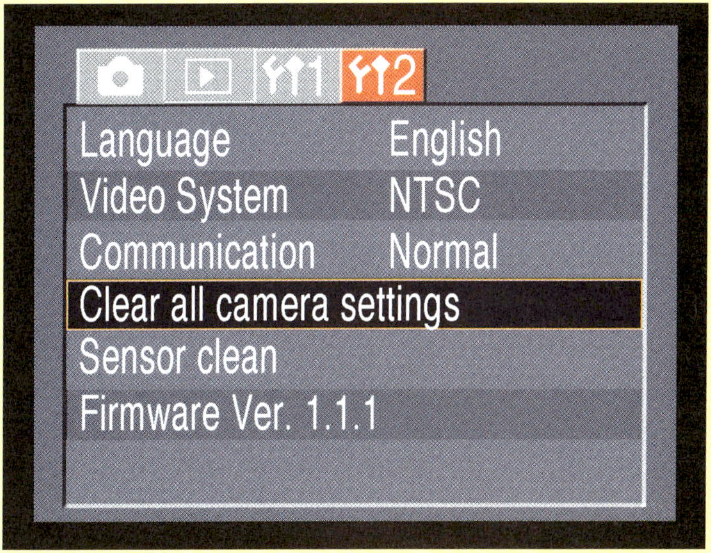

If you've messed with so many settings on the camera that you have no idea where you are (or where you're going) you may want to reset the camera to the original factory defaults (so it's just like opening the camera again for the first time). To clear all your settings and revert to the default settings, start by switching the Mode Dial to the one of the Creative mode settings (like A-DEP, M, Av, Tv, or P), then press the Menu button on the back of the camera. Press the right arrow button three times to toggle over to Set-up Menu 2, then use the down arrow button to scroll down to "Clear all camera settings." Press the Set button, and the factory defaults are restored.

Using the self-timer

> *Want to shoot a shot with you in photo? Use the self-timer*

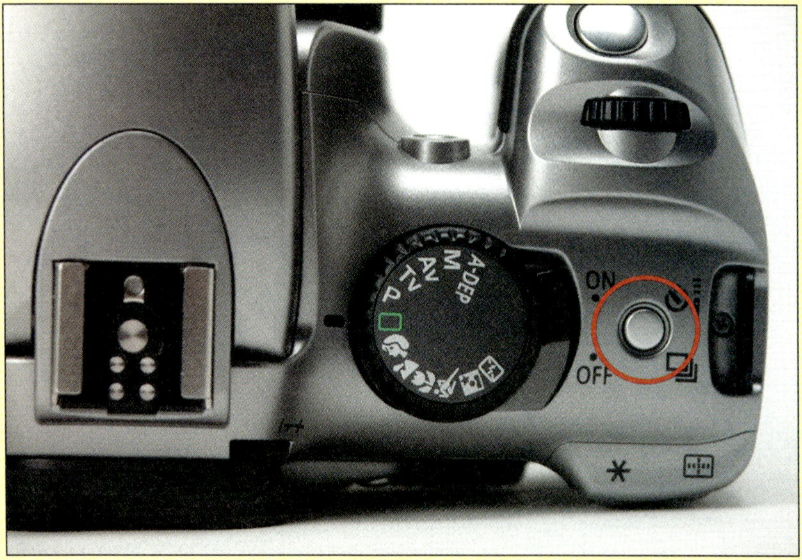

If you want to take a photo so that you're in the photo (rather than being behind the camera taking the shot), you can use the Digital Rebel's self-timer. You start by pressing the Self-Timer button on the top of the camera, just to the right of the Mode Dial (it's circled above). Then press the Shutter button all the way down to activate the countdown timer. You now have 10 seconds to get into position before the self-timer snaps the photo. Once you press the Shutter button, you'll hear a beeping sound (to let you know the self-timer has been activated). When there are only 2 seconds left before it shoots, the beep gets much faster, letting you know it's time to "smile," and then it takes the photo. By the way, if you decide you want to cancel the self-timer once it's engaged, just press the Self-Timer button again. To return to regular shooting, press the button one more time.

Where to go to learn more

> *Canon's online learning center should be your next stop*

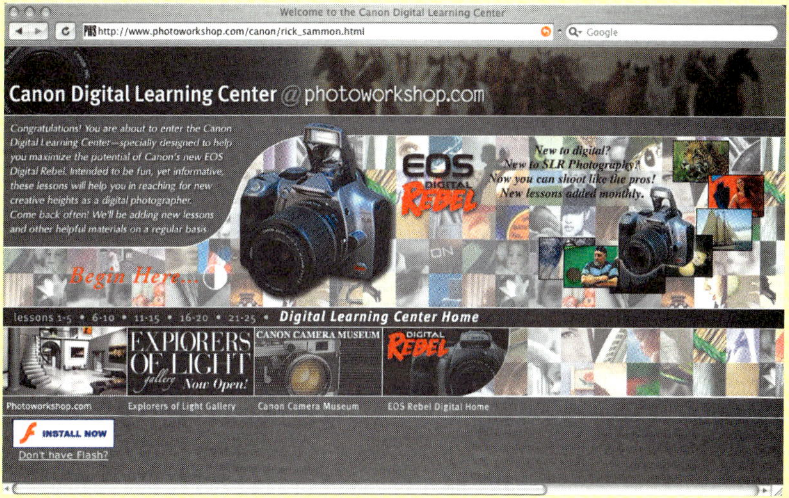

When you're ready to learn more about the Digital Rebel, I highly recommending visiting Canon's Digital Learning Center at photoworkshop.com (the full address is www.photoworkshop.com/canon/rick_sammon.html). You'll find a weath of info on digital photography, including an entire area dedicated to the Digital Rebel.

Index